KT-437-029

# ERNEST

First published 2009 by Macmillan Children's Books
This edition published 2010 by Macmillan Children's Books
a division of Macmillan Publishers Limited
20 New Wharf Road, London N1 9RR
Basingstoke and Oxford
Associated companies throughout the world
www.panmacmillan.com

ISBN: 978·0·230·71255·3

Text and illustrations copyright © Catherine Rayner 2009
Moral rights asserted.

All rights reserved. No part of this publication may be reproduced, stored in or
introduced into a retrieval system, or transmitted, in any form, or by any means
(electronic, mechanical, photocopying, recording or otherwise), without the prior
written permission of the publisher. Any person who does
any unauthorized act in relation to this publication may be liable
to criminal prosecution and civil claims for damages.

3 5 7 9 8 6 4 2

A CIP catalogue record for this book is available from the British Library.

Printed in China

| MORAY COUNCIL LIBRARIES & INFO.SERVICES | |
| --- | --- |
| 20 32 16 68 | |
| Askews & Holts | |
| JA | |
| | |

For Abigail
and Alastair

. . . and tiny Isabella too x x

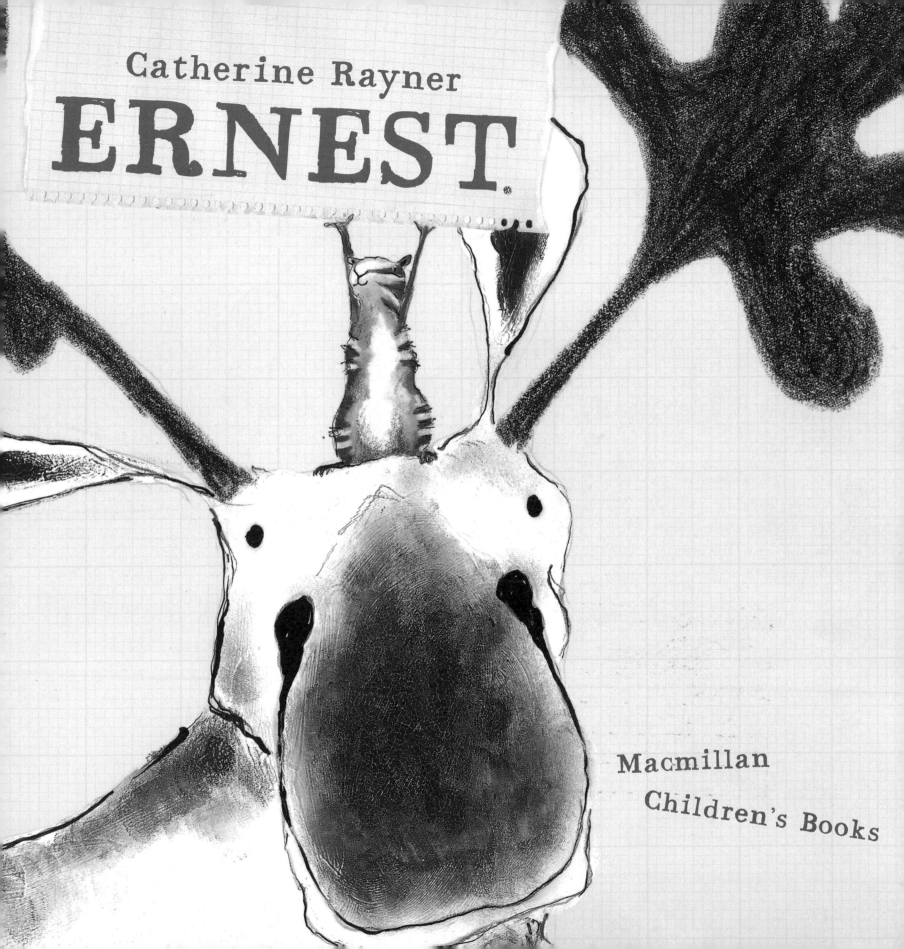

Catherine Rayner

# ERNEST

Macmillan

Children's Books

Ernest is a
RATHER
LARGE
moose.

He is so

# LARGE

that he can't fit
inside this book.

Luckily, Ernest is also
a very determined
moose. He's not going
to give up easily.

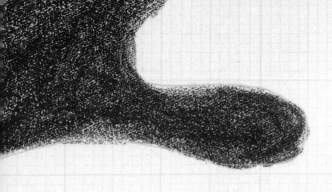

He struggles to

# SHIMMY,

# SHUFFLE and

# SHUNT

in forwards.

He tries to

# SQUIDGE,
# SQUODGE
and
# SQUEEZE

in backwards.

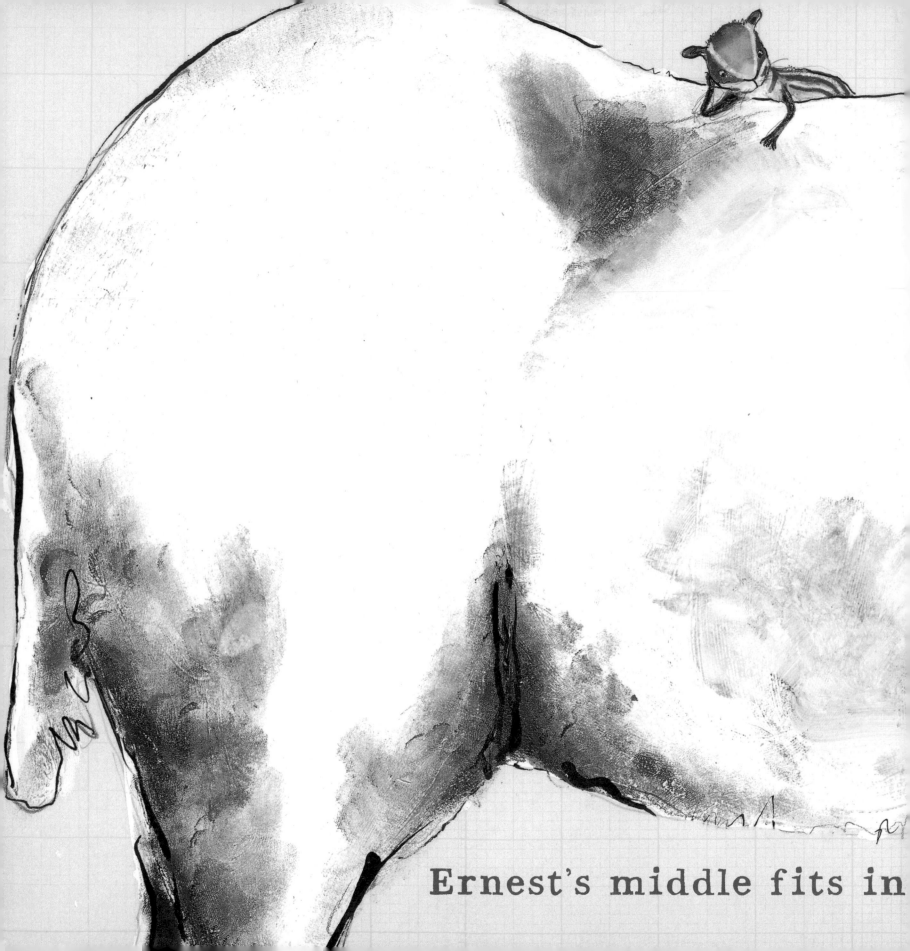

Ernest's middle fits in

easily.

But what about
the rest of him?

Ernest is very
disappointed.

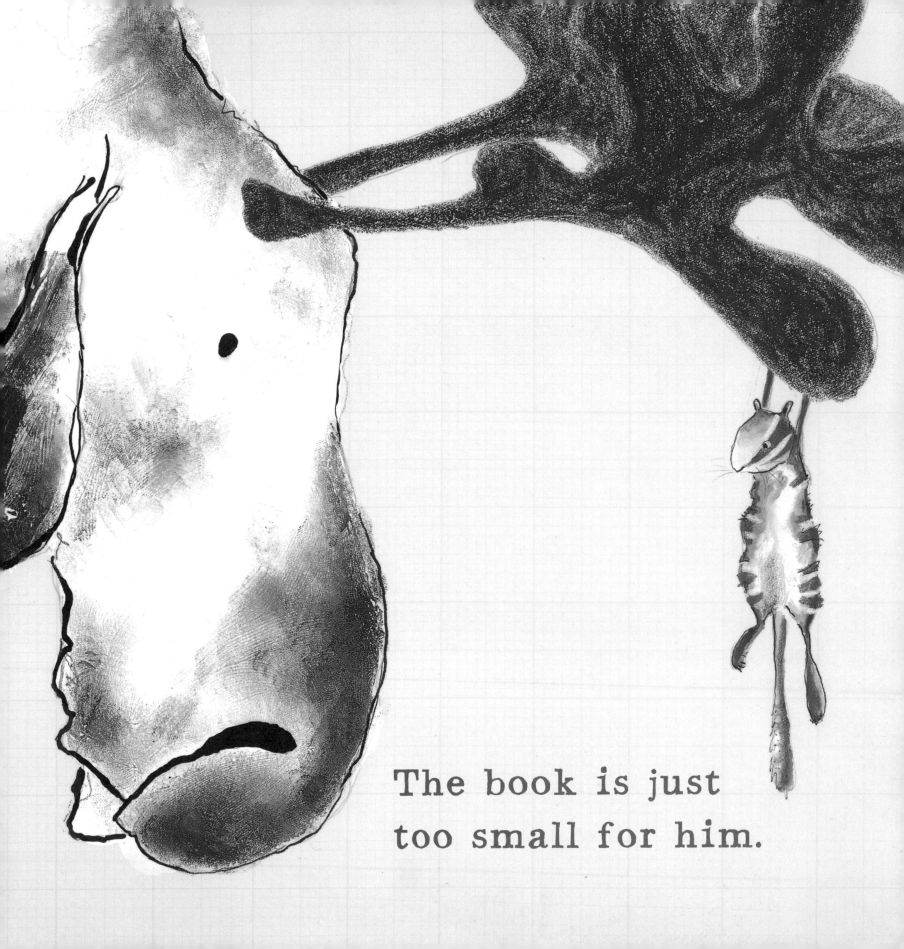

The book is just
too small for him.

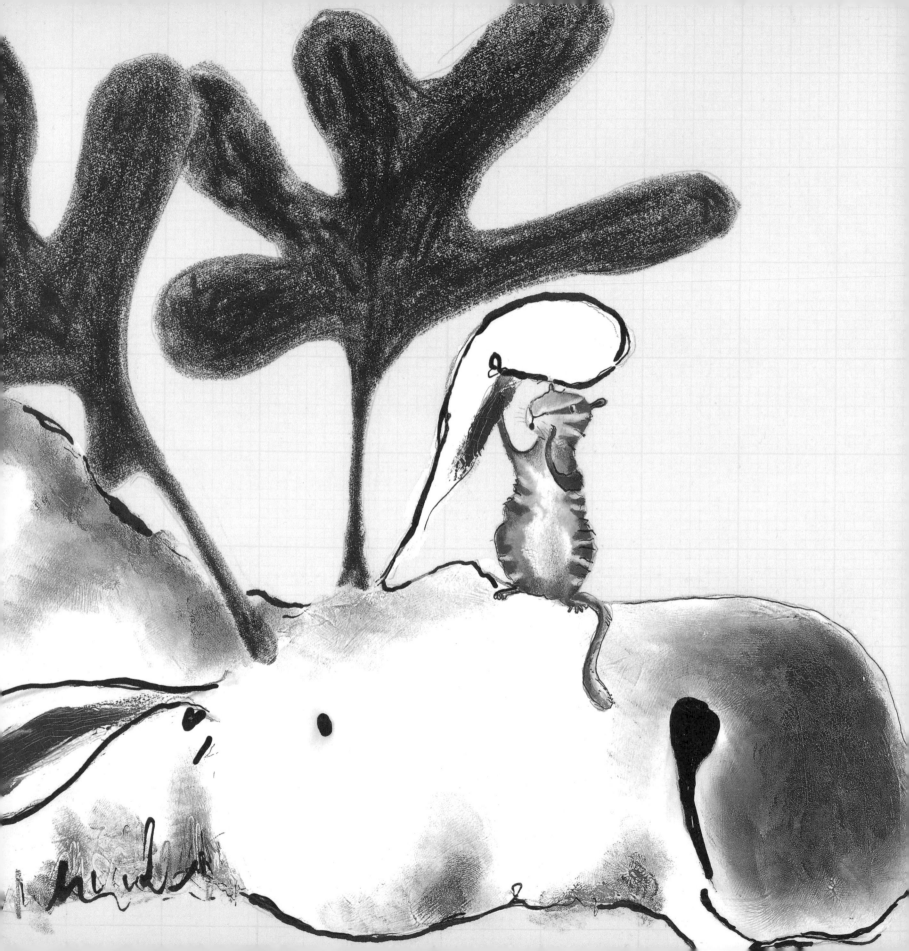

Or is it?

Ernest's little friend
has a
# BIG
# IDEA!

She fetches some sticky tape . . .

and Ernest collects
some paper.

Together they carefully crinkle, scrumple and stick.

They are busy for
a very long time . . .

Finally, they are finished.